A MOUSE STORY

Minnikin, Midgie, and Moppet

BY
ADELAIDE HOLL

PICTURES BY
PRISCILLA HILLMAN

Golden Press • New York
Western Publishing Company, Inc.
Racine, Wisconsin

In a lovely grassy meadow, bright with butterflies and flowers, there lived a happy little family – Mother Mouse and her three little ones, Minnikin, Midgie, and Moppet. They had a cozy mouse house tucked away beneath the roots of an old oak tree.

The little mice played happily in the meadow among the tall grasses, and nibbled on tender green shoots. They dozed in the warm sunshine and ran about in the cool of evening, feasting on delectable weed seeds. They grew sleek and plump on the morsels of grain that lay ripe and golden in the farmer's fields.

Yes, there was just about everything there that meadow mice could ever wish for.

But as the three little mice grew bigger, they began to talk of going off to see the world.

"When I grow up," said Minnikin, "I am going to be a barn mouse. I shall have a little home beneath the sweet-smelling straw in the farmer's barn. I shall eat fat kernels of corn, and delicious grains of wheat."

"When I grow up," said Midgie, "I am going to be a market mouse. I shall live in the village, in a cozy little hole on Market Street, just east of sausages, at the corner of pastries and fine cheeses."

"When I grow up," said Moppet, "I am going to be a house mouse. I shall live an elegant life in a plush city apartment. I shall dine on the finest of crumbs and cheeses and go out to the theater."

Mother Mouse looked fondly at her little ones. "It seems to me," she said, "that the loveliest place in the world for little meadow mice is in the meadow. But then, you are all getting older," she added. "I suppose you will soon be big enough to choose for yourselves."

Days went by, and weeks went by, and months went by. Then one fine morning, when the apples in the orchard were ripe and red, and when the pumpkins in the pumpkin patch were round and golden, Minnikin, Midgie, and Moppet went to talk to their mother.

"We have decided to go out into the world to seek our fortunes," they said.

Mother Mouse kissed them gently. Then each little mouse set off into the wide world all alone.

Minnikin hid in the pumpkin patch until the last
golden pumpkin had been loaded onto the farmer's
wagon. Then he scrambled aboard and hitched a ride to
the big red barn on the hill.

Midgie crept softly to the vegetable garden. He watched and waited as the farmer loaded his truck for a trip to the village marketplace. Then he stowed away quietly among a truckload of turnips, and potatoes, and melons. "Soon I shall be a market mouse and have a wonderful time for myself," he said.

Moppet waited, still as a mouse, in the corner of the garage while the farmer's wife and children got into the car for a trip to the city. Then Moppet slipped behind the back seat of the car. "I'm on my way at last," she said. "I shall be a very fine house mouse in a very fine house."

Days went by. Mother Mouse lived quietly in her little house in the grassy meadow. She was not one who cared to travel. She had never been more than a field or two away from home. But it was lonely with her family gone. So one day she thought, "I really should see a little more of the world myself. After all, I'm not getting any younger. I shall visit Minnikin in the red barn."

The next afternoon she left home in the meadow and traveled all the way to the farmer's big red barn on the hill.

Minnikin was delighted to see his mother. He showed her all over the shadowy, sweet-smelling barn. Together they explored the hayloft, the mangers, and the little secret places under the floor.

Then Minnikin led his mother to a wonderful storehouse filled with sacks of grain. They were just settling down to a feast of corn when there was a sudden rustling of wings. Something with great gleaming eyes and a sharp beak and pointed claws began to swoop down from the rafters.

Mother Mouse gave a frightened little squeak.

"Look out!" cried Minnikin. "It's the barn owl!"

They ran into the mousehole. "Don't be afraid," said Minnikin. "That old owl hasn't caught me yet, and he never will!"

But Mother Mouse didn't hear him. She kept right on running, like a streak, out the door, down the hill, and all the way back to her home in the meadow. There she curled up, trembling with fright. "I will never again leave my cozy meadow home," she said.

15

But after a few days had gone by, Mother
Mouse had almost forgotten her fright. "Besides,"
she said to herself, "it would be good to see a little
more of the world. There must be so much more
beyond the red barn. I shall visit Midgie at
the market."

So off she went to market.

Midgie greeted his mother happily. He led her through a tiny hole into a snug little house under the floor.

"See my beautiful home," he boasted. "I can sit in my doorway and smell the fresh, sweet pastries baking in the great ovens of the patisserie. I can listen to the sharp, quick strokes of the meat cutter's knife as he slices sausages. Then after the shops are closed, I can creep out and feast on the most delectable of foods."

Toward evening, when the lights were out in the market place, Midgie led his mother out the tiny door. They scuttled over the cobblestones to the meat cutter's shop. They were just about to begin nibbling on a bit of fine sausage when a black shape crept across the floor. Mother Mouse looked up to see a pair of green eyes shining in the darkness. She began to shake and quake with fear.

"It's the market cat," whispered Midgie. "He doesn't scare me. I can outwit him. Let's make a dash for my doorway."

18

Mother Mouse made a dash, but not for the doorway. She went like the wind, out of the market and into the street. She ran, and ran, and ran. She did not stop running until she was back home in the meadow.

She huddled in her bed, in a frightened little ball. "This time I am sure I have seen quite enough of the world beyond the meadow," she said.

But the next morning, after a good sleep, Mother Mouse began to think. "I really should see the city once in my life. Besides, I should like to know how Moppet is getting along."

She set off along the highway,
keeping well out of the way of cars, and
traveled a long, long way–all the way
to the city.

23

Moppet welcomed her mother with a kiss. "Let me show you my fine city home," she said. "I am an apartment house mouse. I live in one of the best places on Park Avenue."

Cautiously Moppet led her mother past the doorman. Tucked into a corner of the elevator, they rode up, up to the very top floor.

"Tonight," announced Moppet proudly, "we shall dine on English muffin crumbs, caviar, and blue cheese."

She led the way into a pantry that smelled spicy and delicious. Mother Mouse sniffed with delight. Then she followed her nose toward the wonderful scent of fine cheese. She was just about to take a nibble when Moppet pushed her roughly aside. "Look out, Mother Mouse!" she shouted. "Don't you know a mousetrap when you see one?"

Mother Mouse looked puzzled.
"No," she said, "I have never seen a
mousetrap. There are no mousetraps in
the meadow."

"Well, I'm too clever to get caught
in one of those things," bragged Moppet.
"I've learned to stay away from them.
Now, let's taste these delicious crumbs."

But before Mother Mouse could
take a nibble, a light flicked on.
Someone screamed, "Get out of here,
you pesky mice!"

SWAT! Something crashed down
dangerously close to Mother Mouse.

"Run!" called Moppet. "It's the
broom!"

28

Mother Mouse ran under the table with Moppet close behind. "Don't worry," said Moppet. "I'm very good at dodging brooms. The people will leave soon and we can have our fine dinner. Just wait a minute, Mother Mouse."

But Mother Mouse did not wait–not for a minute, not even for a second. She dashed out the door and into the hallway. She didn't wait for the elevator but ran down twenty flights of stairs, all the way to the street. Her heart was pounding like a tiny hammer.

She darted in and out, trying to stay clear
of people's feet. She dodged here and there, very
narrowly escaping the car wheels that whizzed past.
She ran on and on.

At last, very tired and quite
out of breath, she stopped to sleep
at the edge of the highway.

When Mother Mouse
awoke, rain was falling steadily.
She shivered with cold and set
off again. "If ever I get home,"
she said, "I will stay in the
meadow for the rest of
my days."

Mother Mouse traveled on and on. After a while, the rain stopped and familiar places began to appear. There was the farmer's cornfield, with the cornstalks marching in tall, straight lines. She scuttled quickly between the rows.

Just beyond the cornfield lay the
pumpkin patch. As she darted through the
wet pumpkin vines, a dark shadow fell across
her path. Mother Mouse crouched motionless
beneath a pumpkin leaf. A large hawk
wheeled overhead, then flew on.

Mother Mouse peered
cautiously from behind the leaf.
Just beyond the field she saw the
old oak tree and her house.

"Safe at last!" thought Mother Mouse. Then she took a closer look. There was something in the grass by the roots of the old oak tree.

"The old meadow snake!" thought Mother Mouse as she started to run. "I'm not as quick as I used to be, but maybe I can make it."

WHISK! Mother Mouse raced through the tiny door just as the snake reared its head to strike. She tumbled in a quivery little heap on her soft bed. "Even in the meadow there are dangers," she thought. "And I am not as young and as clever as I used to be. Oh, it is good to be home!" she murmured. Then she fell fast asleep.

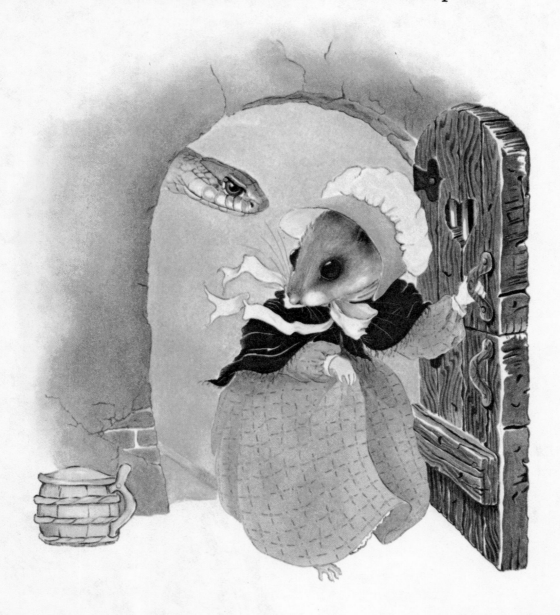

Days went by, and nights went by. November winds whistled down the chimney of the little house, but Mother Mouse was snug and warm inside.

Then one evening there came a small knock at the door. Mother Mouse ran to open it. There stood Minnikin, speckled with snow and looking a little like a snow mouse.

"I decided to come home and see how you were managing all by yourself," he told his mother. "Besides, I didn't like being a barn mouse all alone."

"Welcome back," cried Mother Mouse.

Days went by, and weeks went by. Then one cold January day when snow sifted down over the meadow, there came a tiny *rap, rap* at the door.

"Come in. Come in," called Mother Mouse. And who should come in but Midgie, with frosted whiskers and snow on his tail.

"I thought maybe you needed some help, Mother Mouse," he said. "I liked being a market mouse, but I like being in the meadow with you even more."

"I'm glad you've come home," said Mother Mouse.

Days went by, and weeks went
by. Then one cold day in February,
when the bare trees creaked and
swayed in the bitter winds, Mother
Mouse looked up from her work to
see a little, whiskery face peering
in the window.

"Moppet!" she cried excitedly,
"you're back!" And she rushed to
let her in.

Now that her family was all together again,
Mother Mouse had a fine tea party with delectable things
to eat. Then they all settled down, cozy and contented,
through the winter days and nights.

One sunshiny day, when the meadow was bright with butterflies and flowers, Minnikin, Midgie, and Moppet went to talk to their mother.

"I think," said Minnikin, "that it is time we had homes and families of our own."

"I think," said Midgie, "that we should settle down here in the meadow."

"I think," said Moppet, "that we have seen a great deal of the world beyond the meadow and we have learned to take care of ourselves. Now we can help take care of our mother."

Days passed, and weeks passed, and months passed. And after a while, in the green, grassy meadow there lived, not one, but four happy little families in four cozy little mouse houses in the roots of the old oak tree.